I never wipe it clean
I just sniff and snuff about.

SNIFF, SNIFF,
SNUFF, SNUFF,
SNIFF AND
SNUFF ABOUT!

I'm a dirty dinosaur
with a dirty face.

I never have a wash
I just shake about the place.

SHAKE, SHAKE,
SHAKE, SHAKE,
SHAKE ABOUT
THE PLACE!

I’m a dirty dinosaur
with a dirty tum.

I splatter it with mud
and I tap it like a drum.

TAP, TAP,
TAP, TAP,
TAP IT LIKE
A DRUM!

I'm a dirty dinosaur
with dirty, dirty feet.

I splash in all the puddles
and I stamp about the street.

STAMP, STAMP,
STAMP, STAMP,
STAMP ABOUT
THE STREET!

I'm a dirty dinosaur
with a dirty tail.

I flick it in the muck
or I slide it like a snail.

SLIDE, SLIDE,
SLIDE, SLIDE,
SLIDE IT
LIKE A SNAIL!

I'm a dirty dinosaur.
I'm YUCKY! Oh, my gosh!

I think I'll stomp right to the swamp
And . . .

. . . give myself a wash!

WASH, WASH,
WASH, WASH,
GIVE MYSELF
A WASH!